The
PLANT
SITTER

The PLANT

by GENE ZION

HARPER & ROW, PUBLISHERS

SITTER

Pictures by **MARGARET BLOY GRAHAM**

NEW YORK AND EVANSTON

"I'm a plant sitter!" said Tommy.

"That's nice, dear," said his mother.

"Tell me about it later.

I'm going shopping and I'll be back soon."

When Tommy's mother came home, she got
the surprise of her life. The whole house was full
of plants and Tommy was still bringing in more.
"What's going on here?" she gasped.

"I told you," answered Tommy. "I'm a plant sitter.
I take care of plants for people who are away
on vacation. All the neighbors are my customers."
"Oh, my," groaned his mother. "How terrible!"

When Tommy's father came home, he tripped
over a plant. "What's this nonsense?" he roared.
"Remember?" said Tommy.
"You said I could do whatever I liked this summer

because we weren't going away on vacation."
Tommy's father nodded. He remembered.
"Well," said Tommy, "I'm a plant sitter and I get
two cents a day for each plant I take care of."

Tommy took good care of the plants.

He put those that needed shade on the shady side—

and those that needed sun on the sunny side.

He watered them carefully—
some a lot—and others just a little.

He was such a good plant sitter that in a few weeks
the plants grew into a tangled jungle!

Each night his father said, "This can't go on!"
But it did. And Tommy thought it was wonderful.

In the morning when the family had breakfast,
they were surrounded by plants in the kitchen.

It was just like having a picnic in the woods!
But Tommy's father didn't seem to enjoy it at all.

Watching television in the living room was like being
at an outdoor movie deep in the heart of the jungle.

Tommy thought it was the greatest fun he'd ever had.

But his father grumbled more than ever.

Even the bathroom was full of plants.

Having a bath was like swimming in a little lake

in the middle of a beautiful forest.

But one night Tommy almost fell asleep in the tub.

Plant sitting was hard work and he was tired.

"You'd better go to bed, dear," said his mother.

"You've got to get up early and water those plants."

Tommy went to bed and fell asleep
wondering when his customers were coming home.
He began to dream.

He dreamed the plants grew so thick and wild
that he couldn't get into the house any more.
He had to water them through the chimney!
All night he dreamed that they grew and grew.

They grew so big and strong
that the house came apart and the sides fell down!

All the neighbors ran around shouting,

"Where are my plants? Where are my plants?"

Tommy awoke with a jump. It was morning.
His father was late for work and shouting,
"Where are my pants? Where are my pants?"
"Oh, what an awful dream!" thought Tommy.

He didn't even finish his breakfast that morning.
"See you later!" he called to his mother
as he rushed out of the house.

Tommy ran all the way to the library
and looked at every book they had about plants.
Finally he found just the right book!

Then he ran to the plant supply store,
bought some things and hurried home.

When he got home, he did what the book said to do.

He cut and trimmed all the plants.

It was just like giving them a haircut!

Then he planted the cuttings
in the little flower pots he'd bought.
The book said they would grow.

When the neighbors came home from vacation,
they paid Tommy and took their plants back.
"How nice they look!" everyone said.
"How healthy they are!"

Tommy gave baby plants to all the children,
and everyone went home feeling very happy.
There wasn't a single plant left in the house.
Tommy thought his father would be very happy too.

But after supper Tommy got a surprise.

"Do you know," said his father, "I miss those plants.

It was like being in the country when they were here."

Then he lit his pipe and said, "I'm not so busy now.

How about a vacation after all? We all need one."

"Especially me!" shouted Tommy.

And the very next day they went to the country.